P9-DNN-771

First published in English by Creative Editions in 2000

123 South Broad Street, Mankato, MN 56001 USA

Creative Editions is an imprint of The Creative Company

Text and Illustrations © 1998 by Editions du Seuil

Translation © 2000 by The Creative Company

Original title: Le Train Jaune   Printed in Belgium

Library of Congress Cataloging-in-Publication Data

Highet, Alistair. [Train jaune. English] The yellow train / written by
Alistair Highet; based on a story by Fred Bernard; illustrated by François Roca.
Summary: A young boy takes an adventurous journey with his grandfather
on the old train, recalling how it was used to explore and settle the Far West.

ISBN 1-56846-128-3

[1. Railroads-Trains-Fiction. 2. Grandfathers-Fiction.] I. Roca, François, ill. II. Title.

PZ7.B45505 Yg   2000   [E]-dc21   99-045318

First Edition   2 4 5 3 1

Written by **ALISTAIR HIGHET**   Based on a story by Fred Bernard   Illustrated by **FRANÇOIS ROCA**

THE YELLOW TRAIN

CREATIVE ⚘ EDITIONS

One dark night I went on a strange and wonderful journey. I boarded a train, unsure of where I was going and more unsure of what might happen.

As I traveled, I tried to sit quietly and read my book, but the train was crowded and I was nervous. Suddenly, with a hiss of steam, we came to a screeching halt inside a vast station.

"Last stop! New Caldera!" The conductor shouted. "End of the line!"

I had no choice but to grab my bag and jump off the train. Hundreds of people were hurrying this way and that, pushing and pulling. I didn't know where to turn.

Then I saw a familiar face in the crowd. "Grandpa!" I shouted as I ran toward him.

"Hello, Theo," he laughed, waving to me. "Did you have a good trip?"

"Grandpa! Grandpa! I'm so happy to see you. What are you doing here?"

My grandfather picked me up and gave me a big hug. "I'm here to take you on a special journey. Are you ready?"

"Sure, Grandpa! But where are we going?"

"No time for questions, son. We've got to hurry."

Grandfather took my hand, and we walked down to the far end of the long platform. There, behind one of the Big Blue Trains, was a smaller Yellow Train.

Grandpa stood near it, beaming with pride. "This is my train."

"*Your* train?"

"That's right. A long, long time ago, before you were born, I was the conductor on this Yellow Train."

"It's a beauty," I said, touching the yellow paint.

"When I was a young man," my grandfather continued, "I drove this train to the most wonderful places. I haven't driven it in years. But today, Theo, we're going to take it out for a spin."

11

I could barely contain my excitement as we climbed aboard. Grandpa reached into his pocket, pulled out a set of long, shiny, yellow keys and quickly started the engine. With a lurch and a blow of the whistle, *Toot! Toot!*, the train began to chug slowly down the tracks.

"Watch what I do," Grandpa shouted over the noise of the engine. "You need to learn this."

I nodded and watched carefully as he worked the controls.

"Now, Theo," my grandfather said, looking over the top of his nose, "this trip is going to be like none other you've ever taken. But no matter what happens," he shouted as the train roared out of the station, "this is our secret!"

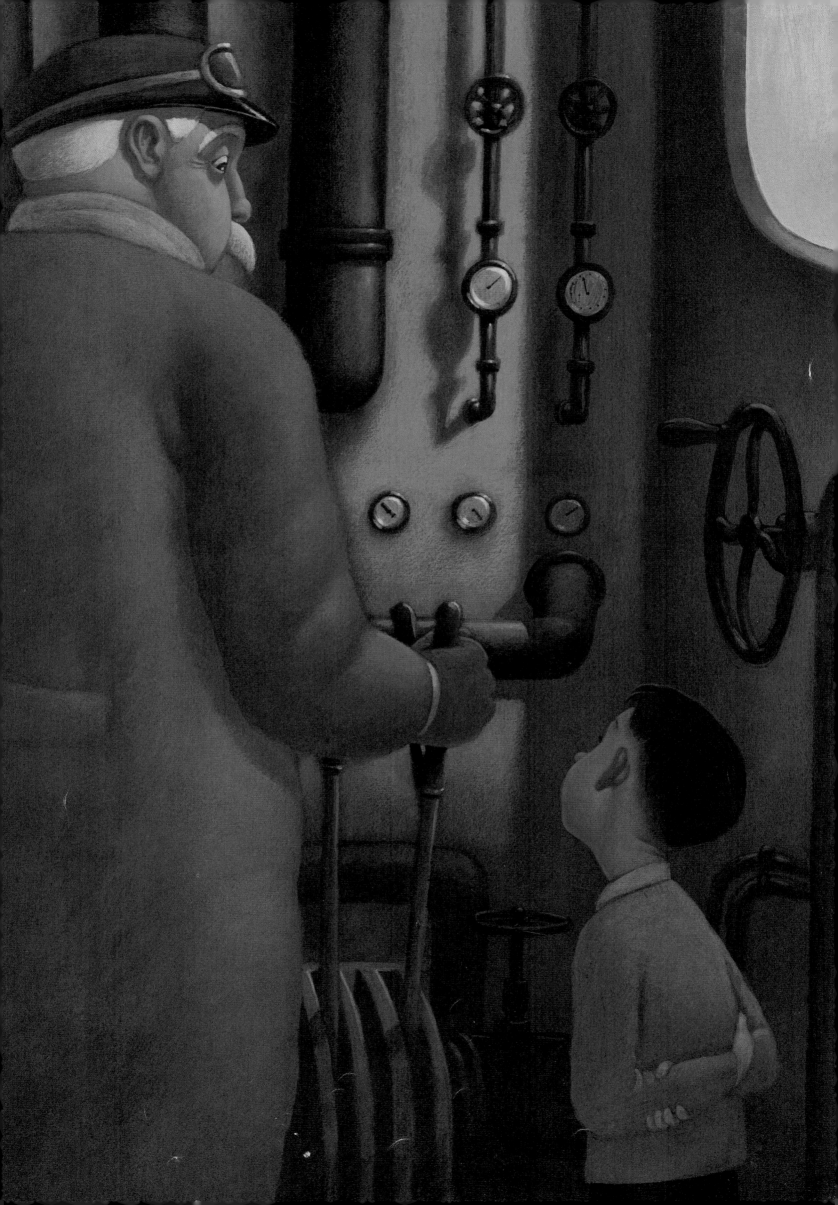

In what seemed like no time at all, we left the city behind. The Yellow Train raced along a stretch of green valley. High mountains towered on each side of us.

"Where are we?" I asked.

"We're at the very beginning of the world," Grandpa roared with happy laughter. "When I was young, not much older than you, I drove this train from coast to coast. The country was unspoiled then. No tall buildings, no huge freeways, and no Big Blue Trains. Only mountains and rivers and the wide wind-swept prairie."

W e left the valley, and the Yellow Train began a slow climb into the snow-covered mountains. I stuffed my hands in my pockets to keep them warm.

"I was the first train conductor to come into these mountains," grandfather said. "I rode the Yellow Train to the top of the world." With that the train shuddered and came to a violent stop.

"Not again," Grandpa muttered. "Guess we're stuck."

"What are we going to do?" I asked.

And then I saw it. Loping toward us was an enormous, hair-covered creature. It looked almost human, but it was the size of at least ten men. "Grandpa! It's coming right at us!"

"Don't be afraid, Theo. It's the Yeti—an old friend."

"Nice to see you again," Grandpa shouted as he stepped out of the train. "Think you could give us a push?"

When the Yeti nodded, Grandpa climbed back on board. The creature gave us a shove and the train began to chug along the tracks again.

"Wow!" I exclaimed. "Mom's never going to believe this."

My grandfather smiled. "Now, Theo, remember what I said?"

We descended quickly through the low foothills and soon found ourselves in a dense, green jungle. The air grew heavy and humid as the train followed the twisting tracks between towering trees. Bright-beaked macaws and emerald-colored quetzals peeked at us through the leaves and vines.

"Keep your eyes peeled," Grandfather said.

The shrill sounds of birds and jungle beasts echoed all around us as the Yellow Train snaked through the darkness.

"You never know what to expect in here," he added.

No sooner had Grandpa said that, then *whoosh!* We shot out of the jungle and onto a high bridge spanning a crowded city. A Big Blue Train came speeding past us with a terrific blast of air.

"This all used to be jungle," Grandpa sighed as we rattled through the city. He seemed bewildered. "Where did it all go?"

"We're so high up," I said. "I feel dizzy."

"Sudden changes can make us feel that way," my grandfather responded.

Then, as quickly as we had entered the city, we left it behind. Not long after we reached the plains, Grandpa pointed over my shoulder. "Look behind you! It's the Snake People!"

They galloped toward us, kicking up clouds of dust, faster and faster. Both wonderful and terrifying, they chased us, singing out their fierce battle cries. *Whoop! Whoop!*

"They're getting closer," I shouted, clutching my grandfather's arm. "They're going to catch us."

"Don't worry," Grandpa said. With that he opened the throttle and the Yellow Train shot forward.

"**W**ow," I said as we traveled farther across the plains. "That was a close one."

"Not *that* close." Grandfather beamed with pride at his Yellow Train and patted the gear box with his gloved hand. "She always was a fast train," he said.

"Why were the Snake People chasing us?" I asked.

"This is their land," he explained. "They see the Yellow Train bringing strange new things to their country and they want to slow it down."

As we rode along, Grandpa recounted some of his other journeys. The Yellow Train had carried everything from ice to coal to elephants!

"That was a quite a day," Grandpa said, "when we arrived with the circus in New Caldera. The Yellow Train was so exhausted after the trip across the mountains, and with such a heavy load on board, that she gave up on the outskirts of town. She just ran out of steam."

"What did you do?" I asked.

"It was simple," he said with a laugh. "We got the big elephants out of the train and hitched them to the front. With a brass band thundering and the whole town cheering, those animals towed the Yellow Train right down Main Street."

Traveling down the tracks, listening to my grandfather's voice, I studied his smiling face. He seemed to grow younger and younger as we flew along. His moustache turned from white to brown, and his cheeks became flushed.

"All right, Theo," Grandpa said, "it's your turn."

"My turn?"

"That's right, you take over now." Grandpa guided my hands onto the levers.

"Hold her steady, boy." My grandfather laughed, leaning out of the window, his scarf fluttering behind him in the breeze. "This is just like the old days," he said. "I was young and carefree, and the thing that made me happiest was to drive my Yellow Train."

"Like now?" I asked.

"Yes, Theo, but..." his face grew sad and tired "...something unexpected happened."

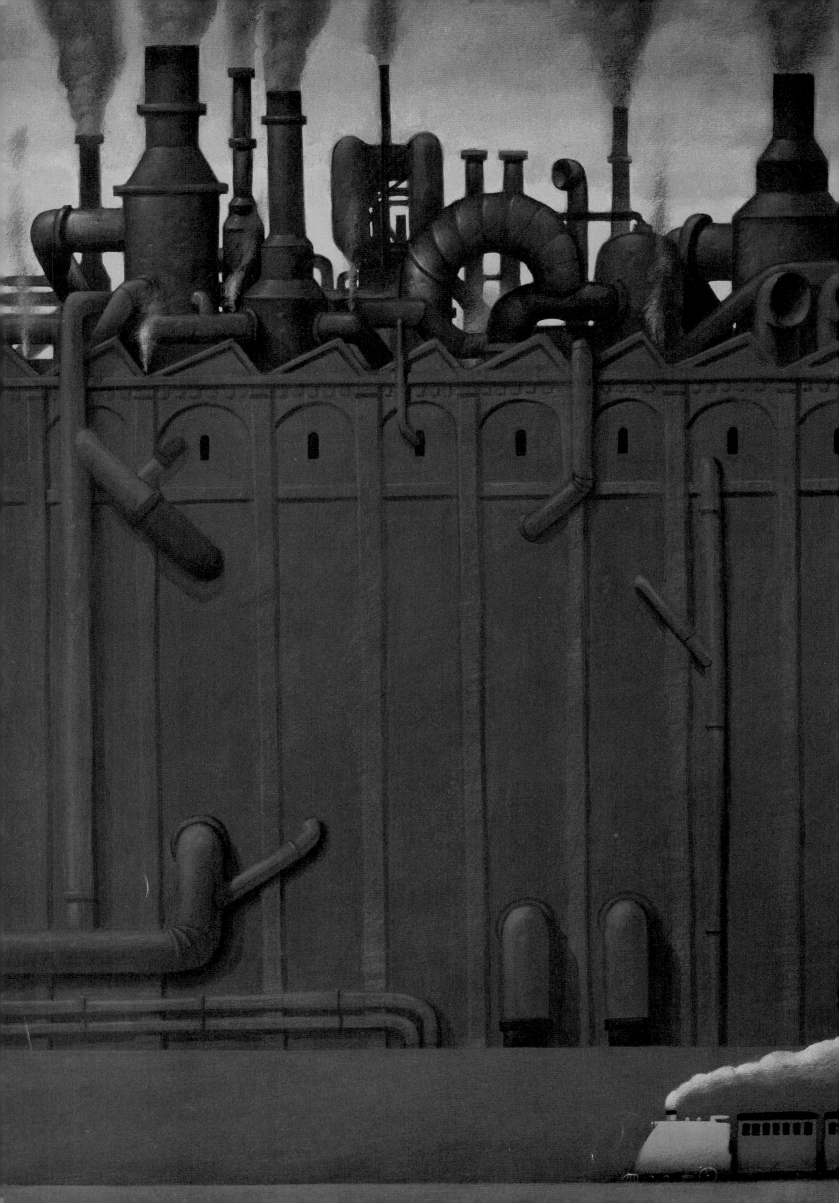

We suddenly found ourselves back in New Caldera. The Yellow Train slowed as we passed beneath a massive factory with towering smoke stacks. The Yellow Train seemed small and powerless under the building's great shadow.

"You see, Theo," said Grandpa. "This is what happened." He pointed at the giant wall of rusting iron. "The factories came and divided up the countryside. Without even knowing it, my work was destroying areas of the plains and valleys and mountains that I loved so much."

I didn't understand. "How?" I asked.

"In my Yellow Train, I carried men and materials—lumber and iron and nuts and bolts—to build the new cities. I brought machines and tools into the wilderness. They used the iron and steel that I brought across the ice and snow of the mountains to build the factories—and even the Big Blue Trains.

"Then one day they told me they didn't need the Yellow Train anymore." My grandfather sighed. "That was my last journey."

The Yellow Train slowed down as we approached the station. My head fell against Grandpa's arm.

"So that's why I wanted to take you on this journey, Theo. I wanted you to see the world that I saw when I was a young man—not so much older than you. A world of grassy fields and snowy mountains, of prairies and green jungles."

"Can't we go back?" I asked him. "I don't want to stay here."

Grandpa shook his head. "There's no going back for me—I'm too old for that kind of adventure. But *you* can go any time you want." Grandpa put his hand on my shoulder. "I'm giving you the Yellow Train, Theo."

"To me?"

"That's right. It belongs to you now. I want you to take it out on new adventures. I want you to find new mountains and new plains and new jungles. They will be your stories."

Then the train hurtled into the long tunnel of the station, plunging us into complete darkness.

I'm still not sure what happened that night with Grandpa, but when Mom came into my room the next morning she woke me with a shout: "Theo! Where did you get those keys?" I opened my hand and saw them too. "Those look like your grandfather's keys," she said. "The keys to his Yellow Train."

They certainly *were* his keys...and I still have our secret.

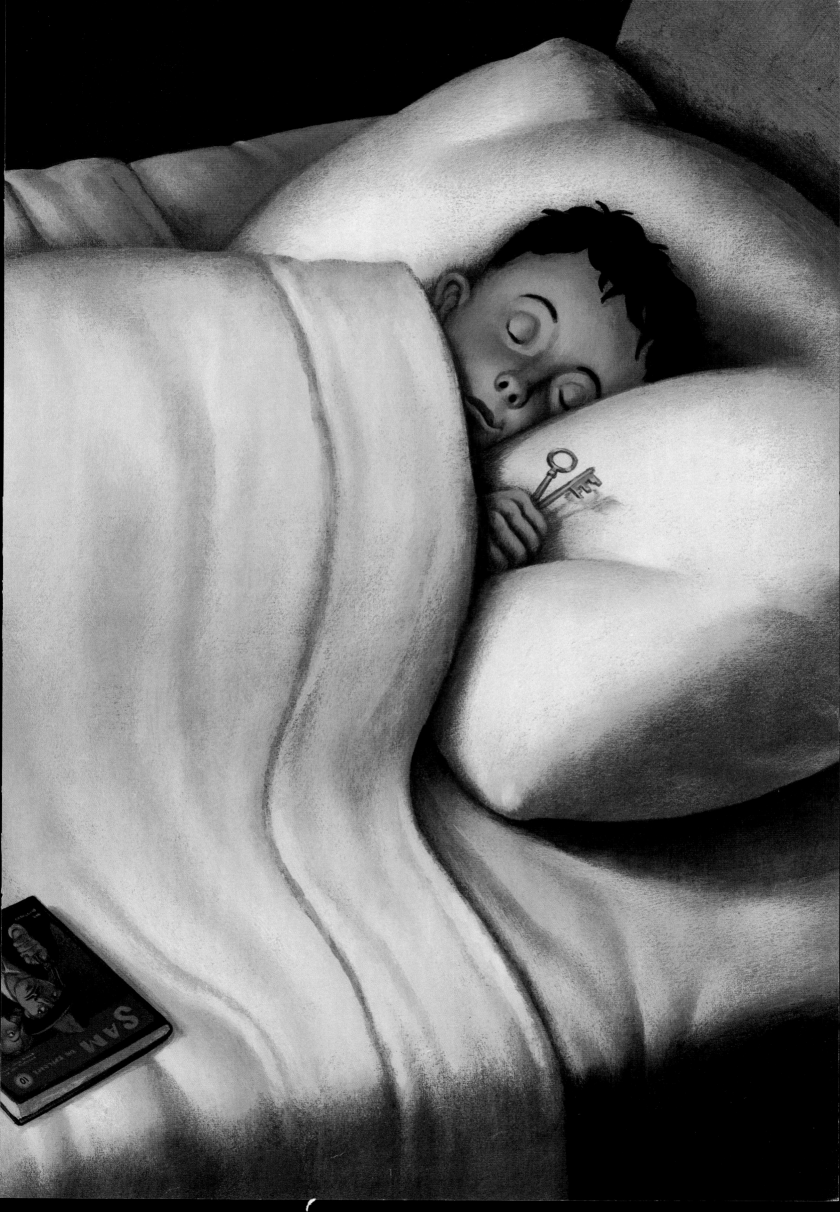